38x 6/12 9/12 11/15 50x 9/15

D0458865

THE AMERICAN GIRLS

  1764 **KAYA**, an adventurous Nez Perce girl whose deep love for horses and respect for nature nourish her spirit

  1774 **FELICITY**, a spunky, spritely colonial girl, full of energy and independence

  1824 **JOSEFINA**, a Hispanic girl whose heart and hopes are as big as the New Mexico sky

  1854 **KIRSTEN**, a pioneer girl of strength and spirit who settles on the frontier

  1864 **ADDY**, a courageous girl determined to be free in the midst of the Civil War

1904 **SAMANTHA**, a bright Victorian beauty, an orphan raised by her wealthy grandmother

  1934 **KIT**, a clever, resourceful girl facing the Great Depression with spirit and determination

 1944 **MOLLY**, who schemes and dreams on the home front during World War Two

 1974 **JULIE**, a fun-loving girl from San Francisco who faces big changes—and creates a few of her own

1974
MEET
Julie
An American Girl

By MEGAN McDONALD

ILLUSTRATIONS ROBERT HUNT

VIGNETTES SUSAN McALILEY, GEORGE SEBOK

★ American Girl®

Questions or comments? Call 1-800-845-0005, visit **americangirl.com**,
or write to Customer Service, American Girl, 8400 Fairway Place,
Middleton, WI 53562-0497.

Printed in China
07 08 09 10 11 12 LEO 10 9 8 7 6 5 4 3 2 1

PICTURE CREDITS

The following individuals and organizations have generously
given permission to reprint images contained in "Looking Back":
p. 81—Photo by Bettye Lane; pp. 82–83—Patti Huntley (young Katy Steding);
ABL Photos (basketball game); Library of Congress (Edith Green);
© Bettmann/Corbis (Jackie Adams); Jo Freeman (buttons); pp. 84–85—© IOC/Olympic
Museum Collection (Olympic medal); *Sports Illustrated* (Billie Jean King); © Bettmann/Corbis
(Sally Ride); pp. 86–87—courtesy *Ms.* magazine; © Bettmann/Corbis (Nixon headlines);
p. 88— © Tore Bergsaker/Sygma/Corbis (Mia Hamm)

Cataloging-in-Publication Data available from Library of Congress

FOR RICHARD

Table of Contents

JULIE'S FAMILY

JULIE
*A girl full of energy
and new ideas, trying to
find her place in
times of change*

TRACY
*Julie's trendy
teenage sister, who is
fifteen years old*

MOM
*Julie's artistic
mother, who runs
a small store*

DAD
*Julie's father,
an airline pilot who flies
all over the world*

IVY
*Julie's best friend,
who loves doing
gymnastics*

T.J.
*A boy at school
who plays basketball
with Julie*

COACH MANLEY
*A gym teacher
who coaches the
basketball team*

MOVING DAY

The world spun—first upside down, then right-side up again—as Julie Albright and her best friend, Ivy Ling, turned cartwheels around the backyard.

"Watch me do a backflip!" called Ivy. She leaned back, stretching her neck like a tree bending in the wind. Soon her shiny black ponytail bounced upside down as she twirled through the air, landing perfectly on two feet.

"I always fall flat on my face!" said Julie. "I'll never be as good as you, no matter how hard I practice." She sighed. "I'm sure going to miss doing gymnastics with you after school every day."

"I'm going to miss playing basketball in your

driveway," said Ivy, "even though you always beat me."

Julie stuck out her lower lip and made an exaggerated sad face. Both girls fell down laughing. Then they stretched out on the grass, folding their hands behind their heads, and gazed dreamily at the clear blue sky, a perfect September day.

"Hey, look," said Julie, pointing to an airplane high up in the sky. "Maybe that's my dad! Hi, Dad!" The two girls whooped and yelled and waved.

Mr. Albright was a pilot. Julie always waved at every airplane she saw, imagining it might be her dad flying to some exotic, far-off country.

"What are you going to miss most?" Julie asked.

"Walking to school together and sitting behind you in class," said Ivy. "Passing notes and braiding your hair when the teacher's not looking." Julie had long, straight blond hair, and Ivy could make a teeny tiny braid down one side in seconds.

"Who am I going to be lunch buddies with?" said Julie. "You're the only friend in the world who would trade me your Twinkie for a pickle!"

"Julie!" Mom called from the back porch as she took down some hanging geraniums. "Time to get a move on. The van will be here in half an hour."

Julie and Ivy turned cartwheels all the way to the back steps. "I guess I better get going," said Ivy.

"Not yet!" said Julie. "Come up to my room with me while I make sure I'm all packed."

Upstairs, Julie scooped up Nutmeg, her pet rabbit, from her favorite spot in the laundry basket and plopped down cross-legged next to Ivy on Mom's old footlocker. It was covered with travel stickers of Big Ben, London Bridge, and the Eiffel Tower. Ivy stroked Nutmeg's velvet-brown fur, while Julie scratched her pet behind her floppy lop ears. Nutmeg snuffled softly, and her sleepy eyes started to close. "I'm sure gonna miss you, girl," said Julie, kissing her on her wiggly nose and nuzzling her whiskers. "But Ivy's going to take extra-special good care of you whenever Dad's gone."

Julie took a long last look around her room. Ghosts of posters that had once decorated the walls formed an empty gallery around the room, showing off the flowered wallpaper. Craters in the blue shag rug made a strange moonscape, a map of where Julie's desk and dresser had once been. Boxes were piled up everywhere.

"It looks like a fort in here," said Ivy.

"Remember when we built that fort out of clay we dug up from the garden? And we dressed up our Liddle Kiddles in old-timey clothes."

"I remember," sighed Ivy. The room turned middle-of-the-night quiet. Julie and Ivy couldn't look at each other.

"I still can't believe you're moving," said Ivy, flashing her dark eyes at Julie.

"It's only a few miles away, across town," said Julie. "It's not like I'm moving to Mars."

"I won't be able to blink lights at you from across the street anymore to say good night," said Ivy.

"But we can call each other up," Julie pointed out. "And you'll still see me on the weekends when I come visit my dad." There was that lump again. She felt it every time she thought of being without Dad. She thought she'd gotten used to the idea of her parents being divorced, but now that she wouldn't be living with Dad anymore, suddenly it wasn't just an idea. It was real.

"Here," said Julie. "I made us friendship bracelets. We can both wear them, and think of each other." She handed a colorful knotted bracelet to Ivy.

"Neat!" said Ivy. "And it's red and purple, my favorite colors."

"Red and purple are my favorites, too," said Julie. "Also blue, green, pink, and sometimes yellow!"

"Put it on my ankle," said Ivy, holding out her foot. "Hey, do you have a Magic Marker?"

"What for?" asked Julie, taking out a pen from her box of desk stuff.

"Give me your foot," said Ivy.

Julie held out her once-clean high-top sneaker. She had doodled all over it with markers. Ivy wrote something on the rubber tip of the toe. Julie peered at the letters: A. F. A.

"A Friend Always!" said Julie.

Julie's big sister, Tracy, poked her head into Julie's room. "Mom says to start bringing our stuff down. Set it in the front room."

"Not yet!" Julie protested. "Just a few more minutes." It was bad enough they were making her move. Now they were taking away her last moments with her best friend, too.

"Mom says *now*," said Tracy, sounding annoyed.

Julie got up and tried lifting a too-heavy box,

then set it back down and began dragging a garbage bag across the floor instead. "Now I know why they call it Labor Day," she grumbled.

"I guess I better go, for real this time," said Ivy. Julie nodded. The two friends hooked pinkies in a secret handshake they'd had since kindergarten. Neither girl wanted to be the one to let go first.

❖

Julie, Tracy, and Mom sat cross-legged on the floor of their new apartment, holding cardboard cartons of Chinese takeout. Mom had pushed a few moving boxes together to serve as a table, and their dinner was spread out on top of the boxes.

"It's so great here," said Tracy. "I found this cool stairway you can climb up at Farnsworth. You can see all the way to that new skyscraper that looks like a pyramid." She paused to slurp some noodles off her chopsticks. "And you should see all the groovy shops I passed along Haight Street when I went to get the takeout!"

Julie admired the way Tracy was always so confident about everything. She wished she

could be certain she'd like it here.

"My favorite part is that we live above the shop now," said Mom. "Think of it! To go to work, I just have to run downstairs!"

A few months ago, Mom had opened a shop downstairs at street level, on the corner of Redbud and Frederick, with windows that faced both streets. Mom's shop was full of handmade stuff, such as purses made of worn-out blue jeans. The shop was called Gladrags. Mom had told Julie it was from the Rod Stewart song that went "*the handbags and the gladrags . . . *" The name was Tracy's idea. She had

7

heard the song on the radio.

"How about you, Julie?" asked Mom. "What do you think you're going to like best about living here?"

Julie glanced around the room. Tiny rainbows of color danced across the empty walls, flashing from the prism Mom had hung in the front window.

"Well, um, I especially like the dining table," Julie decided, pointing to the boxes they were eating on. Mom and Tracy laughed.

"The real dining table isn't put back together yet," said Mom. "I couldn't find the screwdriver."

"Couldn't find the hairbrush, either, huh, Mom? Have you looked in a mirror lately?" asked Tracy.

To Julie, her fifteen-year-old sister was a teenage hair freak. Tracy actually used orange-juice cans for curlers to straighten her hair! Julie looked over at her mom's tumbling brown hair, held in a sagging bun with a pair of hair sticks. "Tracy's right, Mom. You should see— you have a big giant hair bump!"

"More like a camel hump!" said Tracy. The two girls leaned back, laughing.

"Hey, what can I say?" asked Mom. "It's hard to

look like Miss America on moving day." Mom's bangle bracelets jingled as she tried to pin her hair back up.

The doorbell rang, and Tracy ran to answer it. "Mom, it's some guy," she announced.

Julie looked up from her chicken chow mein. Standing in the doorway was a curious-looking man. He had a bushy red beard and wiry red hair, and he wore a patched green army jacket and a baseball cap.

"Hank!" said Mom, standing up. "C'mon in. Girls, this is Hank, a friend from the neighborhood. He was my first customer the day I opened the shop!"

"Far out," said Tracy.

"Hank, these are my girls, Tracy and Julie."

"I've heard a lot about you from your mom," said Hank. "Here." He held out a plate covered with foil. "I made you some of my famous zucchini bread, to welcome you to the neighborhood."

"Yum!" said Julie and Tracy, peering under the aluminum foil.

"Thanks," said Mom. "Can't wait to taste it. Can you stay for some tea?"

"No, I'm on my way to a big meeting about the Vet Center. But thank you." He handed Mom the foil-

9

covered plate, tipped his cap at Tracy and Julie, and left.

"That was so nice of him," said Tracy.

Mom nodded. "Hank's a good egg." She set the plate on the kitchen counter. "Now, where were we? Let's get this footlocker into your room, Julie."

"You're going to help me fix up my room, right?" Julie asked.

"Of course, honey."

"I need curtains," said Julie. "And a lampshade for my light."

"We can make curtains," said Mom. "And decorate a lampshade. Hey, how would you like one of those fuzzy rugs in the shape of a foot?"

"Perfect!" said Julie, helping Mom clear away the leftovers.

"I volunteer to wash the dishes tonight!" said Tracy.

"There aren't any dishes," said Julie. "We ate out of the boxes."

"Exactly!" Tracy grinned. She pretended to practice tennis against the living-room wall with a fake racket—first her forehand, then her backhand. "Did you guys know that back in the olden days, before they even had rackets, people used to play tennis with their hands?"

"I had no idea," said Mom.

"I just can't wait for school. I'm going out for the tennis team. Maybe debate, too. But definitely tennis," Tracy chattered on. "Someday I want to go to France. To the French Open."

"What's that?" Julie asked.

"It's only a world-famous tennis match. Chrissie Evert won the Grand Slam there for the last two years in a row!"

"My sister's a hair freak *and* a tennis freak," Julie announced.

Tracy pretended to lob the ball right at her sister. "Fifteen–love!" said Tracy.

"I don't see how I'm going to start a new school this week," Julie said when Mom came to tuck her in. "I don't even know where a pencil is, or my binder or anything. What if I left some of the stuff I need at Dad's? What if I get lost trying to find my classroom? What if nobody talks to me and I can't find a friend?"

"Honey, I know this is all new, and it's not going to be easy at first," Mom said, sitting down beside

Julie on the bed. "But I'll take you the first day, and we'll meet your teacher and make sure you know your way around. And how could the other kids not like you?" Mom reached to hug her.

Julie squirmed away. "You don't understand."

"You know, when I was your age, Grandpa moved us to France for a year. I could barely speak French, and I was sure nobody would ever like me."

"What happened?" Julie asked.

"Well, there was this one girl in my class. She kept trying to tell me my dress was pretty, but I thought *'Ta robe est belle'* meant she wanted me to rub a bell! I finally figured out what she was saying, and we had a good laugh. Eventually, we became best friends."

"I never knew you lived in France," said Julie. "So those stickers on your old footlocker are real? You saw the Eiffel Tower in person?"

"Sure did," said Mom. "Look, I know starting over in a new place is scary. It's scary for me, too, starting a new business. But sometimes you just have to trust in yourself and take a chance." Mom kissed Julie on top of her head and turned out the light.

CHAPTER
TWO

CAPITALS AND
CUPCAKES

On the first day of school at Jack London Elementary, Julie missed Ivy every minute of the day. She had to memorize state capitals all by herself in social studies. She had to sit alone at the lunch table, without Ivy to help make up silly names for the strange-looking food—names like Macaroni and Squeeze with Princess and the Peas. And there was nobody to laugh with her on the playground when she spotted a funny poodle wearing a tie-dyed sweater!

Every time she walked down the hall, she found herself looking over her shoulder. Principal Sanchez was all rules and no nonsense. He pointed with a pencil and warned kids to slow down or lower their voices. "Young man, tuck in your shirt!" he told a third grader. "I hope that's not gum you're chewing," he scowled at another student. "One more warning and you'll get a demerit."

Julie soon knew all about Mr. Sanchez's demerit system. Three demerits and you had to stay after school to wash blackboards or scrub desks.

Julie's teacher wrote her name in perfect cursive on the board: Ms. Hunter.

"You forgot the 'r' in Mrs.," a boy in the back row pointed out.

"It's *Ms.* Hunter," she told the class, drawing out the word "mizzz" to sound like a buzzing bee. "Not Miss. Not Mrs."

"Huh?" The students looked at each other, confused.

"Think of it like *Mr.* You call a man Mr. whether he's married or not, right?"

The class nodded silently.

"Well, Ms. is the same thing, for a woman."

"But why?" asked a bold girl named Alison. "What's wrong with Miss or Mrs.?"

"Whether or not a woman is married is her

private business," Ms. Hunter explained. "Ms. works either way."

Julie carefully wrote out "Ms. Hunter" in her best cursive. She wasn't sure she understood. Would people be calling her mother Ms. Albright now?

❧

The only kid who talked to her all day was the boy who sat next to her in class. He had a short mop of sandy hair, a spray of freckles across his nose, and a funny name that sounded like a president. Every time Ms. Hunter called him Thomas Jefferson, Julie had to hold back a giggle. "It's T. J.," the boy corrected her.

When Ms. Hunter told the class to take out their rulers, Julie didn't have one. The girls behind her whispered and twittered. Julie heard the scornful words "new girl" and "divorce." She instantly felt her cheeks get hot. How in the world could they know about that already?

"Don't mind them," whispered T. J. "Amanda, Alison, and Angela. To get into their club, your name has to start with an A."

Julie nodded. The Water Fountain Girls. She'd

seen them hanging around the water fountain that morning, pointing and snickering.

T. J. handed her a ruler. "Here, you can borrow mine. I have an extra."

"Thanks," said Julie. "We just moved, and it's kind of hard to find stuff in all the boxes."

Before T. J. could reply, Ms. Hunter broke in. "Julie Albright. In my class, we don't speak when the teacher is talking."

"But I didn't have a—"

"It's okay this time. But remember, boys and girls. Any talking out of turn is a demerit."

Great, thought Julie. *First day of school and I'm already in trouble.*

Julie sat up straight and opened her math book, but she couldn't help thinking of Ivy starting fourth grade in Mr. Nader's class. At Sierra Vista, her old school, most kids couldn't wait for fourth grade. Mr. Nader let the fourth graders hatch out butterflies right in the classroom!

As Ms. Hunter wrote a metric chart on the board, Julie imagined Painted Lady butterflies flitting and floating around the classroom. She pictured one landing on the top of her teacher's poufy hair. Julie almost giggled

16

at the thought, but she caught herself.

"Class," said Ms. Hunter, "President Ford is about to sign a bill that will soon have the whole country using the metric system. It's what the rest of the world uses. Australia and New Zealand have converted. The metric system is taking over the world, and we Americans don't want to be left behind."

Julie sighed. *Millimeters? Decimeters? What's wrong with good old inches?* she wondered as she picked up T. J.'s ruler. She felt just *inches* away from throwing up her hands in frustration. Or was it *centimeters?*

Every day after school now, Julie came home to an empty house. She was used to having Nutmeg hop right up into her lap the minute she walked through the front door. But because of the stupid no-pets rule at the new apartment, not even Nutmeg was there to greet her. Mom was always busy downstairs with customers at Gladrags, while Tracy had started staying after school for tennis practice.

Three whole days of school had passed, and Julie had settled into a routine. A boring, lonely routine.

Julie picked up the newspaper and opened it to the funnies. She read *Peanuts* first, then her horoscope, just for fun. Tracy was always bugging her, saying, "You don't really believe your fortune will come true, do you?" Julie didn't, but it was interesting to think about anyway. Today, the horoscope for Taurus said:

It's only a matter of time until your feet find the right path.

Now, what was that supposed to mean? Suddenly Julie's stomach grumbled. Maybe it meant her feet were going to find the right path to the fridge for a snack! Julie took out an orange and started peeling it.

Dense gray fog drifted past the kitchen window. Julie shivered. The house was all creepy-quiet, except for unfamiliar creaks and gurgles.

Ivy! Calling Ivy was the best cure for creepy house noises.

"Hi, Poison Ivy," said Julie.

"Hi, Alley Oop! What's up?"

"I haven't seen you for almost a week. I was wondering if you could come over this afternoon."

"You know I can't," said Ivy.

"Gymnastics?" asked Julie, but she already knew the answer.

"What else?" said Ivy.

Julie hesitated, and then asked, "Couldn't you miss gymnastics just this once?"

"I better not," said Ivy. "You know how Coach Gloria always says you don't get to be Olga Korbut and win Olympic gold medals by missing practice."

Julie wished she could go to practice with Ivy, just to have something to do and a friend to do it with. She sighed. "Oh, well, I have a test to study for anyway."

"You have tests already at your school?" asked Ivy. Julie heard a horn honking on Ivy's end. "Gotta go," Ivy said. "I'll see you Saturday. Tests—yuck!"

Julie went to her room, turned on her lava lamp, and spread out her map of the state capitals. *Tallahassee, Topeka, Trenton.* Julie started feeling cross-eyed from staring at all the names and states. She sat up on her bed and looked around her bare room.

Curtains and a fuzzy rug would be a big improvement. *Mom just hasn't had time to help me fix it up yet,* Julie reassured herself. For now, maybe it would help to at least have some of her familiar things around.

Julie opened the old footlocker. She lifted out her basketball and gave it a few friendly bounces. She unrolled the poster of Lucy, from the *Peanuts* comic, that Tracy had given her last Christmas. It showed Lucy with her fist in the air, shouting, "I'm my own person!" Julie tacked it up on her wall.

Next, she took out an envelope and peeled some of her yellow smiley-face stickers off the backing. *They should make frowny-face stickers for days like this,* she thought as she stuck them upside down onto the headboard of her bed. But even upside-down, the yellow smileys annoyed her with their cheeriness.

"Knock, knock," said Tracy, coming in through the bead curtain.

"Nobody's home," Julie answered.

"Someone's in a mood," said Tracy.

"School's hard and I have a test on state capitals and my teacher is really strict," Julie said in one big gush. "But it's not just that. I come home every day and nobody's here, not even Nutmeg. Do you know how many strange sounds a house can make?"

"You can always hang out down at the shop

20

with Mom," Tracy pointed out.

"Mom's busy now. She has customers. She doesn't have time for us anymore."

"Of course she does," said Tracy.

"Not like before," said Julie. "We used to come home and she'd have cupcakes with gooey icing and help with our book reports and stuff."

"Tell you what. How about if I help you study for your test," said Tracy. "I'm a whiz kid when it comes to state capitals."

"I've memorized most of them, except for about twelve that I'll never get. Like Alaska. And Nebraska. And Kentucky."

"All you have to do is make up ways to remember," said Tracy. "Juneau sounds like 'Did you know?' So you think to yourself, did-you-know Juneau is the capital of Alaska?"

"Hey, that's neat!" said Julie.

"C'mon, Jules," said Tracy, standing up. "I have an idea—a place I want to show you."

❀

A bell jingled as Tracy swung open the bakery door, and the warm air was filled with the smell of

21

cinnamon and just-baked cookies.

"Hi, Mrs. Gibson!" Tracy waved. "This is my little sister, Julie, and we've come for cupcakes. One dozen, please!"

Julie and Tracy oohed and ahhed and pointed through the glass to cupcakes with pink and white and lemon-yellow icing. Behind the counter, Mrs. Gibson lined them up in a box and handed the girls some tubes of colored icing.

"You get to decorate your own cupcakes here," Tracy explained.

"Cool!" said Julie. They sat down at a table in the bakery, and Tracy unfolded Julie's map of the state capitals.

"Okay," Tracy started. "There are twelve cupcakes, and twelve state capitals you can't remember, right?"

"Right. But I don't see how cupcakes are going to help me on my test."

"See, we decorate the cupcakes with a picture for each capital. When you go to take your test, you'll be able to remember the picture," said Tracy. "Here, I'll show you. Another name for hot dog is *frankfurter*, so we'll make a hot dog for Frankfort, Kentucky."

She squeezed out pink icing in the shape of a hot dog. "And a little yellow icing for mustard!"

"I get it!" said Julie. "We could do a heart for Hartford, Connecticut."

"And a stovepipe hat for Lincoln, Nebraska," said Tracy.

The fog had lifted, and sun streamed through the bakery window. The bell on the front door jingled, and in walked Hank, unwrapping a scarf from around his neck and taking off his cap.

"Well, if it isn't the Bobbsey Twins," said Hank. "What are you two up to?"

"I'm helping Julie study for a test," said Tracy.

"I don't know," Hank said, stroking his bushy beard. "Doesn't look like homework to me. Julie, you're grinning like the Cheshire cat. C'mon, let me in on the joke. What's so funny?"

"I just ate Lincoln, Nebraska!" said Julie.

JUMP SHOTS AND
REBOUNDS

The end-of-the-day school bell had
rung ten minutes ago, but Julie
lingered at her locker. She was in no
hurry to get home to an empty house again. She
closed her eyes and breathed in the familiar pencil-
shaving and chalk-dust smell, and for just a moment
she was back at Sierra Vista School. But when she
opened her eyes, her locker stared blankly back at
her. Julie pulled the most recent postcard from Dad
out of her book bag and taped it to the inside of her
locker door.

Just as she slammed her locker shut and started
down the hallway, a ball bounced out of the gym
door, off the wall, and against the lockers, and rolled

down the hall, right past her feet. A basketball!

Julie scooped it up and dribbled down the hallway to the gym, glancing over her shoulder to make sure Principal Sanchez was not nearby. A few boys were horsing around at the far end of the court, playing what looked more like dodgeball than basketball. Out of the corner of her eye, Julie saw T. J. bending down, tying his sneaker.

"Think fast!" she called, tossing the ball at T. J. He jumped up, caught the ball in midair, then drove toward the basket. Julie threw down her book bag and followed him down the court.

"Bet you can't get the ball back," T. J. teased, switching from right to left, bouncing the ball back and forth, light on his feet. Quick as a cat, Julie crouched low, sprang forward, and with one clean swipe, snatched the ball away from T. J.

"Good steal," T. J. said as Julie dribbled around him. "You shoot hoops?"

Julie did a layup, then dribbled back over to T. J. "I used to play a lot with my dad."

"Hey, how are you at jump shots? Will you try blocking me on my jump shots so I can practice? I want to play on the school team."

"There's a basketball team here?" asked Julie.

"Yeah. Fourth, fifth, and sixth graders can join. Mr. Manley's the coach. He puts up a sign-up sheet outside his office."

T. J. turned and dribbled hard to the left, but Julie stuck to him like glue. For the next ten minutes, they took turns practicing and defending jump shots, layups, and rebounds.

"Hey, that was boss! Wanna help me again tomorrow?" T. J. asked. "Same time, same place?"

"Really? Sure! That'd be great."

"Okay. Later," said T. J.

"Later," Julie called back.

And for the first time since coming to Jack London Elementary, Julie found herself looking forward to tomorrow.

All week, Julie practiced after school with T. J. Now she'd be able to surprise Dad with some new moves on Saturday. She could hardly wait. Two whole days to see Ivy, play with Nutmeg, hang out with Dad, and sleep in her own room again. It would be just like old times.

First thing Saturday morning, Julie packed her paisley suitcase and waited by the door for Dad to arrive. Tracy came out in orange-juice-can curlers and Miss Piggy flannel pj's, rubbing her eyes as if she had just awakened.

"You better hurry up!" Julie said. "You're not even dressed. Dad's going to be here any minute, and he doesn't like to have to wait."

"I'm not going," said Tracy.

"What do you mean you're not going? It's Saturday. It's our day to go to Dad's and spend the weekend with him."

"Well, I'm staying here. I have tennis practice anyway, and a bunch of us might go see a movie tonight."

"What about Dad? You can't decide not to go, just like that." Julie snapped her fingers. "We're still a family, you know, and Dad's part of it, too."

The orange-juice cans bounced and swung as Tracy shook her head. "Give it up, Julie. We're never going to be a regular family again. This isn't the Brady Bunch. Besides, I'm in high school now. I'm old enough to decide for myself what I do on the weekends."

"You think you're so—" Julie hesitated but couldn't find the right words.

Toot, toot. Dad had said he'd honk for them so he wouldn't have to find a parking place. "He's here!" said Julie. "What am I supposed to tell him?"

"Whatever you want," said Tracy. "I don't care."

Toot, toot, toot. Dad was waiting.

"So you won't care if I tell him my sister turned into an *alien?*" Julie grabbed her bag, ran down the back stairs, kissed her mom good-bye in the shop, and rushed out to the waiting car.

"'*Juu-liaaa, seashell eyes, windy smile,*'" sang Dad. It was his favorite Beatles song, because it had her name in it.

"You look different," Julie told Dad as she got into the car.

"Same old me," said Dad. "So, do you have everything? Where's your sister?"

"She's not coming." Julie looked down, letting her fingernail worry at a scab on her arm.

"But it's our—never mind. Wait here. I'll be right back." Dad sprinted up the steps to the front door. Julie could see him from the back, gesturing with his hands as he talked with Tracy, who stood in her bathrobe with her arms crossed. Finally, Dad came back, without Tracy, and started the car.

He was extra quiet, so Julie tried to think of things to say. She chattered on about her state capitals test, and how all the kids were looking forward to Dad coming to Career Day at school next week, and the new basket she hoped to get for her bike. It would be big enough to hold Nutmeg.

After a few blocks, Julie flipped on the radio and sat back in her seat. She made up her mind to make the most of her weekend with Dad and forget about Crabby Appleton (aka Tracy). Besides, she realized, it might be nice having Dad all to herself for a change.

As soon as they pulled up to the house, Ivy came running across the street. "Alley Oop! You're here!"

"What do you say we head down to the Wharf?" asked Dad, pulling Julie's suitcase out of the trunk. "There's a festival at Ghirardelli Square with face painting, jugglers, magicians, and even a no-hands chocolate-eating contest!"

Julie and Ivy looked at each other with delight. "Can we ride the cable car?" Julie asked.

"Why not," said Dad.

Ivy ran to ask her parents, and soon they were on their way.

Ding! Ding! rang the bell on the cable car. Julie and Ivy hopped up onto the open-air platform while Dad paid the fare. They gripped the pole tightly, hand over hand over hand, and hung their heads out the side, where the wind whipped their hair. Julie let the bright September sun warm her face. Wheeee! The two girls giggled with roller-coaster glee as the cable car barreled down the hill toward the waterfront.

"Blue punch buggy! No punch-backs!" Julie called out, starting off the game she and Ivy played whenever they spotted a Volkswagen bug on the streets of San Francisco. She tapped Ivy on the arm, pretending to give her a punch.

Ivy scanned the cars parked along Hyde Street. "Red punch buggy convertible! I get to punch you twice! No returns!"

"Punch buggy orange!" called Dad from his seat.

"Orange?" Julie and Ivy looked at each other and laughed. "Dad, where do you see an orange VW?"

"That VW van right there," said Dad as the cable car came to a stop at an intersection. "See?" The van was covered with bumper stickers and painted daisies.

"It has to be a Volkswagen *beetle*," said Julie.

"Like Herbie, the VW beetle in the *Love Bug* movie," Ivy explained.

They hopped off the cable car near Ghirardelli Square. Music blared, kites fluttered, and a juggler on stilts amazed the crowd.

"Are those chocolate-covered apples he's juggling?" asked Ivy.

"Look," said Dad. "He's taking a bite from each apple as it goes by!"

Ghirardelli Square

31

Dad spread a blanket on the grass, and they had a picnic on the green, sipping hot chocolate as they watched a mime pretend to climb a flight of stairs.

Ivy told her friend excitedly, "Guess what! On the balance beam, we learned how to do a pike on the dismount."

Julie sighed. "That sounds really boss. I miss going to the Y after school." Then she brightened. "But I had this great idea. I'm going to play basketball. Sign-up is next week."

"That's great, honey," Dad said. "It's nice to have a club to go to after school."

"It's not just a club, Dad. It's a real basketball team, with uniforms and games against other schools and everything."

"I know you'll be a starter on the team," said Ivy. "You're so good at basketball."

"Wow," said Dad. "They have a girls' basketball team at your new school?"

"Not a girls' team. Just a team," said Julie.

"You're joining an all-boys' basketball team?" asked Ivy.

"Why not? T. J.'s my only friend at school, and he's going to play," said Julie. "He says I'm just as good as most of the boys."

Dad put his hand on her shoulder. "Honey, I know you're good, but I've never heard of girls playing on the boys' team. It's a whole different thing playing on a team. It's not like shooting hoops with me in the driveway, or playing a pickup game at the Y. A team can be a lot of pressure."

"It's not pressure to me," said Julie. "It's fun!"

"Well, boys can be super competitive at that age, and they like to roughhouse," Dad continued. "Did you ever think they may not be too happy about having a girl on their team? I'm not so sure it's a good idea, Julie. I don't want you getting hurt."

Julie rolled her eyes. "Da-ad, I'm not going to get hurt! In the newspaper, I saw this picture of a girl from Ohio who got to play on the boys' football team. And football's a lot rougher than basketball." She looked over at Ivy as if to say *Help me out here.*

"Yeah, Mr. Albright. Basketball's probably a lot safer than gymnastics, even," Ivy chimed in.

"Look, honey, I'm just not sure about this. Let me think about it. And I'll need to talk it over with your mother, too."

Once Julie saw the exclamation-point creases

between Dad's eyebrows, she knew it was time to
drop the subject.

❧

That night, when Dad came to say good night
and tuck Julie in, he gave her a souvenir he had
brought back from a flight to Chicago. Julie shook
the snow globe. "What's this?" she asked.

"It's the Sears Tower, honey. It's brand-new, and
it's the tallest building in the world. And I rode up to
the top floor, one hundred ten stories!"

"Wow!" said Julie, watching as miniature
snowflakes settled around the tiny black skyscraper.
What fun it would be to see real snow!

"I have a little something for your sister, too,"
Dad continued, holding out a tennis visor that said
"Chicago" on it. "You'll take it back for me?"

"Sure," said Julie, hunkering down under the
covers. "Don't worry about her, Dad. Mom says it's
just a teenage phase."

"I hope she's right," Dad said.

Julie lifted Nutmeg up onto the bed and
stroked her rabbit's ears. It felt so good to be back
in her old bed. "Dad, you're still coming to school

34

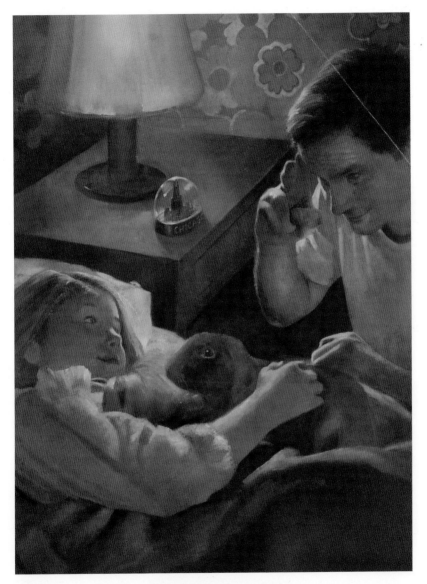

"Pilot's honor," said Dad.

on Monday, right? Like we planned?"

"Of course. It's World's Greatest Dad Day, right? And I'm supposed to wear my pajamas."

"No, Dad! It's Career Day, remember? All the kids in my class think it's so cool that you're a pilot. You have to wear your uniform! And bring everybody those pins of wings they give out on airplanes."

"Okay," said Dad. "I guess I won't wear my pajamas, then."

"Promise?"

"Pilot's honor," said Dad. "Lights out, now. Good night, sleep tight."

"'Night, Dad." Julie waited for a moment. "Dad, you forgot—"

"Don't let the bedbugs bite!" said Dad.

As soon as the lights were out, Julie saw a flash of light in her window, coming from across the street. Ivy was signaling good night with their secret code.

Julie tiptoed across the room to the light switch. She blinked the light ten times in an on-off, on-off Morse code for *Good night, sleep tight, don't let the bedbugs bite!*

CAREER DAY

 On Monday morning, Julie watched the clock, waiting for social studies to be over. The rest of the day would be Career Day, when some of the parents would come to tell about their jobs. Dad was going to tell an exciting story about the time he had to make an emergency landing.

The first Career Day parent was Cathy's dad, a baker who went to work in the middle of the night. He brought two boxes of cream-filled doughnuts for everybody to eat. Kenneth's dad worked at a bank and gave each of the kids a newly minted penny. Robin's dad was a dentist. He gave out special tablets to chew that turned everyone's teeth pink in the places that needed to be brushed better.

Julie was only half-listening as she toyed with her hair, trying to make a tiny braid the way Ivy used to do. It would be Dad's turn any minute. Where was he? Dad was never late—

"Sorry I'm late!" a voice whispered in her ear. Not a Dad voice. *Mom!* What was she doing here? Then, in one heart-sinking moment, Julie knew. Mom had come to break the bad news to her—Dad couldn't be here today.

"Now, our last visitor is Mr. Albright, Julie's father," Ms. Hunter announced. "Mr. Albright is a pilot."

Julie slunk down lower in her chair as Mom made her way to the front, bracelets jangling, and whispered something to the teacher. Then Mom turned and faced the class.

"Hello, fourth grade! I'm Julie's mom, Mrs. Albright. As much as Julie's dad wanted to be here, he just couldn't be. He had to fill in for another pilot who was sick. Right now he's about twenty-seven thousand feet above the Rocky Mountains."

Oh no. This wasn't happening! Julie wanted to

yell STOP, but she froze in her seat while the rest of the class began firing off questions.

"What kind of plane does he fly? Is it a 747?"

"Has he ever been to Hawaii?"

"Did he ever have to make a crash landing?"

"Why is your name Mrs. Albright if you're divorced?"

The room grew quiet. The question hung in the air like fog that wouldn't lift. Julie knew it had to be one of the Water Fountain Girls who had asked it, but she didn't dare turn her head. She stared at a pair of initials carved in her desktop as if it were a work of art in a museum.

"Class," said Ms. Hunter, "remember how we talked about not asking personal questions? Julie's mother has been kind enough to take the time to tell us about her career. So let's give her our full attention. There will be time for questions at the end."

How could this be happening? Julie had bragged to the whole class about the World's Greatest Pilot, her dad. Not her mom, the . . . junk-store lady!

Mom was already pulling a heap of junk out of

39

her old tie-dyed bag. If only Julie could be like Samantha on *Bewitched*, her favorite TV show. One twitch of the nose and she'd blink herself right out of there in an instant. While she was at it, she would blink herself back to her old school. Her old *life*.

"Have you ever wondered," asked Mom, "what to do with old string? A pair of ripped-up jeans? Even apple seeds?"

No, thought Julie. *You throw them away in the garbage!*

Mom began passing around some of the artistic handmade items she carried at the shop, like denim purses, macramé plant hangers, and apple-seed bracelets. Julie looked at the clock. Wasn't that bell *ever* going to ring?

"Did you make that neat bandanna skirt you're wearing?" asked Alison.

"What about this cool blue-jeans purse?" asked Angela, holding it up.

"I like this pink fuzzy foot rug," said Amanda. "It's so cute!"

Julie sat up straight in her chair. The Water Fountain Girls actually *liked* her mom's junk!

"Julie and I just made that for her room," said Mom.

Amanda leaned forward and smiled at Julie. "You made that?" she mouthed, opening her eyes wide and giving her the thumbs-up sign.

"Do you sell Pet Rocks?" somebody asked.

"How about mood rings?" a boy in the front row said.

Suddenly, Julie's whole class had forgotten all about pilots and 747s and crash landings. They didn't even seem to care that it wasn't a dad up there talking. They were bubbling over with questions about what it was like to have your own store.

"I want to own a pet store when I grow up," said T. J. "And have giant lizards and rare albino frogs."

"You mean anybody can just start their own store?" asked Kimberly.

"Sure," said Mom. "I'm not saying it's not hard work. Ask Julie. Some days I'm at my shop until ten o'clock at night. But it gives me a chance to do something creative, and I really like being my own boss."

Mom passed out mood rings and apple-seed bracelets to the entire class.

The students immediately put them on, exclaiming, "Wow!" "Neat!" "You mean we get to keep these? For *free?*"

apple-seed bracelet

"It's called advertising," said Mom. "*Word-of-mouth* advertising. Maybe you'll come to shop at Gladrags now. Or tell a friend."

The whole class clapped when Mom was done. Julie glanced at her mood ring. It had changed from black to blue-green. The chart it came with said blue-green meant relaxed, calm. *Amazing*, thought Julie, realizing that was exactly how she felt.

During afternoon recess, all the kids could talk about was going to Gladrags. They crowded around Julie, asking her when the shop was open and where it was and if she could get stuff for free.

Word of mouth was . . . Julie's *mom* was the coolest parent at Career Day.

❁

"Hey, Julie!" T. J. called, slamming his locker shut from across the hall. "Coach Manley is posting the basketball sign-up sheet after school today."

In her excitement over Career Day, Julie had forgotten that today was the day for basketball team sign-ups. She hadn't even remembered to ask Mom about it. Julie could hardly sit still, waiting for the final bell to ring. As soon as school was out, she rushed down the hall toward the coach's office.

"No running in the halls, young lady!" called Mr. Sanchez. "Even after school." Julie forced herself to slow down.

Coach Manley was a gym teacher. He had buzz-cut hair like a G.I. Joe, a growly face, and a thick neck. Every time Julie passed the gym, he was always shouting.

Julie looked for a sign-up sheet on the wall but didn't see one. She summoned her courage and knocked on the coach's door. She knew just how Dorothy felt knocking at the door of the Wizard of Oz.

"Enter," barked the coach.

Julie fixed on the bump in his nose to steady herself. He reminded her of a dragon, about to breathe fire.

"Hi, Mr. Manley," she said. "My name's Julie. Julie Albright. I'm a fourth grader, and—"

"Yeah, yeah. You looking for the sign-up

sheets? Got 'em right here."

"Really? That's great! So I'm the first one?"

"Yep. How many dozen should I put you down for?" asked Coach Manley.

"Dozen? Dozen what?"

"Cookies. For the basketball bake sale," said the coach, leaning back in his chair. "We're trying to raise money for new uniforms. How about I put you down for some chocolate chip cookies. My favorite."

"Cookies? I'm not here about cookies," said Julie. "I'm here about the team. I want to be *on* the team. The basketball team."

"We don't have a girls' team at Jack London. We can barely afford the boys' team. Why do you think we're having a bake sale?"

Julie took a deep breath. "Not the girls' team. The boys' team."

Coach Manley sat up. She had his full attention now. "Let me get this straight," he said slowly. "You want *me* to put *you* on the boys' basketball team."

Julie nodded, her heart pounding.

Coach Manley smiled and shook his head. "Young lady, the basketball team is for boys, and boys only. Got that?"

"I'm as good as the boys," Julie said softly. "Just give me a chance to try out. Please."

"Sorry. Answer's N-O, no. This is my team and I make the rules. When spring rolls around, we'll have some intramural games—softball, tetherball, badminton. Maybe you can play one of those."

Julie shook her head. "That's not the same." She flushed and looked down at the floor, embarrassed to meet his eyes. A strange new feeling washed over her. It felt like a mixture of shame, frustration, and an emotion she couldn't quite identify.

She glanced up at the coach. He had turned back to his desk, signaling that it was time for her to leave. Her instinct was to run out of his office and never see him again. But something kept her feet firmly planted to the floor.

Finally, Coach Manley looked up. "I have work to do. This conversation is finished."

Julie felt her insides go all runny, like the yellow belly of a breakfast egg. As she turned to go, hot tears smarted at the back of her eyes. Julie swallowed hard, pushing back her fear.

"If there's not a basketball team for girls at this school, you have to let a girl play on the boys' team," she told the coach, her voice shaking. "I read it in the newspaper."

"Did the paper say I don't have to do anything I don't want to do? Case closed. Out of my office."

"It's the law!" Julie whispered, backing away.

"Well, I have a news flash for you, young lady. In this gym, I'm the law." Coach Manley towered over Julie as he leaned across the desk toward her. "Now, do I have to call the principal to escort you out of here? Or will you leave on your—"

Julie didn't wait to hear the rest. She fled. She ran all the way home, wind biting her ears and stinging her cheeks.

❖

At Gladrags, Mom and Tracy had newspaper spread across the table and counter in the back, and they were gluing beads and buttons onto blank white lampshades.

"Hi, honey," said Mom. "I was telling your sister all about Career Day. You just missed some girls from your class. I've already had three new customers since my talk today."

46

Julie wondered if they were the Water Fountain Girls. "That's great, Mom."

"What's wrong with you?" asked Tracy. "Your face is as red as a beet!"

"Wait!" said Julie, looking at the table where they were working. "Are these all the newspapers from last week? Thursday or Friday? I have to find something!" she said frantically, lifting up corners of the newspaper and peering at headlines. "Here it is!" She flipped the paper over to the inside of the sports section, careful to avoid getting stuck with glue, and pointed to the headline: "High School Girl Tackles Boys, School Board."

"See? This girl wasn't allowed to play on the school football team, so she went to court. She won, and they had to let her play, because of this new law."

"Oh, yeah. We learned about that in civics class," said Tracy. "They passed some big federal law to make things more equal."

"I believe it's called Title Nine," said Mom. "But what does this have to do with you, Julie?"

"It's the basketball coach at school," Julie explained. "He won't let me play on the team because I'm a girl."

47

"He's a male chauvinist pig," said Tracy.

"Tracy!" Mom sounded a little shocked. "Where did you hear that?"

"Some people in tennis called Bobby Riggs a male chauvinist pig because he thought Billie Jean King couldn't beat him," Tracy replied. "Then she trounced him in a big match and proved that girls can be just as good as boys in sports."

Billie Jean King

"Look, honey," said Mom, smoothing out Julie's hair. "I don't see why you shouldn't be allowed to play on the team, if that's what you really want. Let's talk this over with your dad when he gets back next week."

"I already talked to Dad about it, and even *he* doesn't want me to play on the boys' team," Julie told her. "But they don't have a girls' team. Besides, tryouts for all the positions are this week. Next week will be too late."

Julie grabbed the page with the article and rushed up to her room. She scooped up her basketball and bounced it against the wall. *Thwump! Thwump!* She knew Mom didn't like her bouncing it in the house, but the satisfying thump of the ball helped ease the bundled-up feelings inside her.

Nobody ever asked her what *she* wanted. Divorce. *Thwump.* Moving. *Thwump.* Changing schools and leaving Ivy. *Thwump-thwump-thwump!* This morning, her horoscope had said "Create your own future by taking charge." Well, taking charge was what she was *trying* to do.

Julie stopped bouncing the ball and sat up straight. She wasn't going to give up. And they couldn't make her!

LET GIRLS
PLAY, TOO

The rest of the week at school seemed to drag on forever. On Friday, Julie was standing in front of her locker at the end of the day when she overheard the Water Fountain Girls whispering to each other.

"Shh! There she is. She's the one," said Alison.

"The one what?" asked Angela. Or was it Amanda?

"Can you believe it?" said Alison. "She actually asked Coach Manley if she could be on the *boys'* basketball team!"

"She's a TOMBOY!" Amanda and Angela hissed, saying the word too loud on purpose.

Julie froze. She stuck her head deeper into her

locker, pretending to look for her reading workbook. A voice came up behind her. "Just ignore them. You're good at basketball."

Julie pulled her head out of her locker and smiled gratefully at T. J. "Does Coach Manley already have his team picked out?" she asked.

"Nope. He's still choosing positions. I'm keeping my fingers crossed I'm a starter. Wish me luck."

"Luck," Julie said longingly, waving goodbye to T. J.

❖

Saturday morning Julie was reading her horoscope—"Don't hesitate; today's the day to jump in"—when she heard Ivy's knock.

"You're here!" Julie said, leading her friend into the living room. The two girls pushed boxes into the corner so that Ivy could show Julie her latest floor routine.

"Did you know Olga Korbut was the first person to do a backward aerial somersault on the balance beam?" Ivy asked as she turned her handstand into a back limber.

Julie tried to copy the move, but as

Olga Korbut

51

soon as she got into a handstand, her feet clomped to the floor.

"Girls!" called Mom. "What's going on? Sounds like a stampede of elephants in there. Julie, please tell me you're not bouncing that basketball inside."

"Don't worry, Mom," said Julie. "It's just handstands."

"Well, I don't want you two breaking your necks, either. Why don't you run down to the deli and get us some lunch meat for sandwiches, and we can have lunch in the shop. I have lots of new beads, if you'd like to make bracelets."

"Ooo, beads!" said Ivy.

"Sure, Mom," said Julie.

As the girls walked down the hill toward Haight Street, Julie told Ivy all about Coach Manley and the basketball team. "After the coach wouldn't let me on the team, Tracy called him a pig," Julie confided.

"Whoa. I'd get in big trouble if I ever called a grownup a pig," said Ivy.

"Not a *pig* pig. A *male chauvinist* pig. It's some big fancy word she learned from a tennis match. It means when boys think they're better than girls."

"I don't see why you'd want to play on a team

with only creepy boys anyway," said Ivy. "They have smelly feet like pigs. Oink, oink!" Julie and Ivy pressed their noses into snouts and couldn't stop snorting and giggling.

At the corner, while they waited for the walk sign, Julie saw Hank. He was carrying a clipboard, going up to cars stopped at the light, and talking to drivers through their car windows.

"Hey," said Ivy, "let's not cross here. Let's go down to the next light."

"But the market's right there," said Julie.

"I know, but I don't think we should walk past that guy," said Ivy, pointing to Hank. "He's weird. He looks like a troll with all that orange hair."

"Oh, that's just Hank. He's a friend of my mom's. I say hi to him all the time."

"I'm not supposed to talk to any strangers," said Ivy.

"Hank's not a stranger. Besides, Mom said I should be nice to him because he's one of those guys that was in the war. A Vietnam vet," Julie explained. "She says it's really hard when you've seen so many terrible, horrible things. Some

53

people just can't get over it."

"Well, I don't know," said Ivy.

The light changed, and Julie took Ivy's hand as they crossed the street. Ivy switched to Julie's other side so that she wouldn't have to walk by Hank. But he had already spotted Julie.

"Hey, how's Lincoln, Nebraska?" he called.

"Great," Julie called back. "I aced my test!"

"Way to go," said Hank, meeting up with Julie on the far side of the street and slapping her a high five. "Who's your sidekick?"

"This is my friend Ivy, from my old neighborhood," said Julie. "We're going to the market to get stuff for lunch. Are you coming by the shop later?"

"No, not today. Too busy." He held out his clipboard. "I still need 81 more signatures."

"Signatures? For what?" Julie asked.

"For my petition," said Hank.

Even Ivy was curious. "A petition?" she asked.

"We're trying to get them to open the Veterans' Center again. That's where all of us vets used to hang out. We liked to go there to chew the fat and play cards, but the center was real important. For some of the homeless guys, it was the only meal they got all day and the only place they had to clean up and stay in out of the rain."

"What happened to it?" asked Julie.

"Same ol' same ol'. Budget cuts. City said they didn't have enough money to keep it open." Hank shook his head. "But we're not giving up. If we each get a hundred fifty signatures, we can take it to the bigwigs at the next board of supervisors meeting, and they have to open the issue back up for discussion."

"I sure hope you get enough signatures," said Ivy.

"Can anybody make a petition?" asked Julie.

"Sure," said Hank. "It's a great way to get people to pay attention to your issue."

"And even if they said no about something, the petition might get them to change their minds?"

"Yep, that's what it's all about," said Hank. "Well, I gotta book," he said, tapping his clipboard. "Check you later."

"Bye, Mr. Hank!" Ivy waved.

"See you later, alligator," called Julie.

As the girls ate their sandwiches, all Julie could think about was starting her own petition. After lunch, while Ivy began stringing glass beads to make a bracelet, Julie drew columns on paper with T. J.'s ruler and numbered the lines up to 150, just like Hank's petition.

"C'mon, Julie," said Ivy. "Don't you want to make bracelets? I'm going to make one for every day of the week!"

"Not right now," said Julie. "I'm making a petition." After all, her horoscope had said today was the day to jump in, so that's what she was doing. Julie wrote "Let Girls Play, Too" across the top of the page and drew basketballs and high-top sneakers in the margins. When she was done, she put on her roller skates.

"Hey, where are you going? I'm only up to Wednesday!" said Ivy.

"We can make bracelets any time," said Julie, waving her papers in the air. "C'mon, I need your help to get people to sign my petition."

Ivy put down her beads and trudged out the door after Julie, calling, "Wait up!"

Julie stopped at the corner. "Let's go ask that lady carrying the groceries across the street."

"For real? You're just going to walk right up to

a perfect stranger and start talking to them? And tell them you want to be on a boys' basketball team?"

Julie felt her stomach do a nervous flip-flop. Maybe Ivy was right. Could she work up the courage to just walk right up to a total stranger? "Please, Ivy, just come with me."

"I don't think my parents would like me doing this," Ivy said.

Julie couldn't help wondering what her dad would say if he knew she was starting her own petition. She pushed the thought out of her mind. "Just help me get started," she pleaded. "I'll do all the talking, and if you don't like it, we can go home. I promise."

Ivy bit her lip. She did not look happy, but she followed her friend across the street.

"Excuse me," Julie called to the lady, who was putting groceries into her trunk. She held out her clipboard for the woman to see. "Would you like to sign my petition? So I can be on the basketball team at my school?"

"Sorry, not interested," said the lady, looking annoyed.

"See? What did I tell you?" Ivy mumbled.

"Let's try that man coming out of the bakery," said Julie. "Hello! Would you like to sign my petition?"

"I'm in a hurry," said the man. "Good luck."

"Boy, he didn't even give me a chance to say what it's for!" said Julie, trying not to feel discouraged.

"How about that lady with the stroller? Maybe she likes kids," Ivy said.

Julie skated up to the lady and started off with, "Oh, what a cute baby!"

"Thanks," said the lady, beaming.

Julie held out her clipboard and explained her petition as the lady rocked the stroller back and forth.

"It's about time they started letting girls play the same sports boys get to play," said the lady. "Where do I sign?"

"Thanks a lot!" said Julie. "You're my first signature."

"I can see that. Well, best of luck to you."

"She was nice," Julie told Ivy.

"Good. Now can we go back and finish making bracelets?"

"Ivy, that's only *one* signature. I need to get a hundred fifty."

Ivy stopped. "A hundred fifty! That could take a year!"

"C'mon, it's not that bad. At least let me get a few more. Hey, there's Hank—I bet he'll sign it."

Julie skated all over the neighborhood with Ivy trudging loyally behind. Every time the girls passed someone, Julie stopped and talked about her petition. Each time, it was like stepping out onstage at a school play, worrying she'd trip over a prop or forget her lines. But for every few people who wouldn't sign or didn't want to be bothered, Julie would find one who agreed with her.

Finally, Julie had almost one full column of signatures. She held up the clipboard triumphantly. "Look! Let's get just a few more."

"You've been saying that for hours," said Ivy. "Why can't we go back now and play Clue, or listen to Tracy's records, or do something *fun?*"

"I can't believe you think this is boring," said Julie.

"We've been doing this all afternoon," Ivy

complained. "I hardly ever get to see you anymore, and I thought we were going to have *fun*."

Julie looked down at her petition. She had collected seventeen signatures, plus three blisters on her feet. She still had one hundred thirty-three more signatures to go. "Well, it's not dark yet, so I'm staying out a little longer."

"But you promised," said Ivy. "You said if I helped you get started, we could go home."

Julie threw her hands up in exasperation. "Don't you want my petition to work? You're my best friend. Don't you care if I get to play on the team?"

Ivy shrugged. "Not if it means we have to keep doing this."

Julie spun around to face her friend. "How can you be so selfish?"

"Because you think playing basketball with a bunch of dumb old boys is more important than being friends with me!" Ivy turned and stomped off.

"Where are you going?" called Julie, skating after her.

"What do you care?" asked Ivy. Ivy's back was stiff as she stormed straight up the hill, faster than Julie could follow on skates.

"What about our sleepover?" Julie called after her. But Ivy turned the corner and disappeared from sight.

The next day, Julie woke up exhausted. Her legs ached and her head felt as heavy as a bowling ball. Her first thought was that she should be having strawberry whipped-cream waffles with her used-to-be best friend Ivy at that very minute. Instead, she sat up in bed and blinked back hot, angry tears.

Why was Ivy being so stubborn? Why couldn't she understand? What if somebody had told *her* she couldn't do gymnastics anymore?

Suddenly, Julie felt furious—at everything. If her parents hadn't divorced, she wouldn't have had to move. If she hadn't moved, she wouldn't be going to a new school with a basketball team that didn't allow girls. She'd have spent her Saturday at the Y with Ivy instead of asking people to sign a stupid petition . . .

The petition! Julie leaped up and snatched the clipboard from her desk. She yanked out the first sheet, the one with all the signatures, and *whhht!*

She ripped the page right in half, and threw it on the floor.

Julie pulled on sweats and sneakers, grabbed her basketball, and ran outside. She dribbled—*bam bam bam*—hard and fast against the sidewalk.

"Hey, you're gonna wear a hole in the sidewalk, Sport!" called Hank, walking up Redbud Street.

Julie turned away and kept dribbling. Hank set down his coffee and bagel bag, came up behind Julie, and stole the ball right out from under her.

"Hey!" Julie chased after Hank, who dribbled down the sidewalk and juked right, then left, trying to fake her out. He spun into a driveway and lobbed up a hook shot as he passed under a rusty basketball rim attached above the garage.

"Nice shot!" said Julie, forgetting her mood. She scooped up the rebound and went for a layup herself.

"Back at you!" said Hank.

They played hoops for several minutes, until Hank flopped down on the curb. "Haven't had my coffee, or I'd be able to keep up with you," he teased.

Julie perched on her ball, catching her breath.

"So, how's the petition going, Sport? You on that basketball team yet?"

"Huh," Julie snorted. "I don't even care about that anymore. It's too hard getting signatures and they'll never let me on the team anyway and besides, I lost my best friend over it," she said in one breath.

"Oh, so you don't mind not being on the team, then?"

Julie shrugged. "Doesn't matter. It's too late, anyway. I ripped up the petition."

Hank raised his eyebrows but said nothing. He gathered up his coffee and bagel and started to leave, then turned back to Julie. "Hey, you remember President Nixon?"

"Sort of. I remember when he resigned from being president," Julie said. She also remembered her parents arguing about him, but she didn't say that.

Hank nodded. "Well, I sure wasn't his biggest fan, but I remember he once said, 'A man isn't finished when he's defeated, he's finished when he quits.'" With that, Hank turned and headed up the street.

Julie went back up to her room and stared at the torn petition. She desperately wanted to be Ivy's friend again. But what would Ivy think if she knew

Julie had torn up the very signatures she had dragged Ivy along for hours to get? Maybe Hank was right. What would she gain by giving up now?

Pushing the two halves back together, Julie smoothed out her petition, then opened her desk drawer and took out some tape.

❦

Now Julie carried the petition with her everywhere she went. She talked to people on her way to school. She asked the teachers, librarian, and school nurse if they'd sign. And she spent every free minute after school going up and down the neighborhood, asking every person who would stop and listen to sign her petition.

But it just wasn't the same without Ivy. When a lady with a parrot on her shoulder signed the petition and the parrot mimicked, "Sign here! Sign here!" Julie knew Ivy would have split her sides laughing. And when she reached one hundred signatures, she had no best friend to jump up and down with.

The next day after school, Julie sank into a chair without even taking off her coat. She banged her clipboard down on the workroom table.

"Why the long face?" asked Mom.

"I've been out there with my petition for over an hour and not one single person would sign it today."

"Any time you try to change something, it's going to be difficult," Mom said gently. "Not everybody thinks girls should play sports. A lot of people think games like football and basketball are just for boys."

"But that's not fair," said Julie.

"I know, honey. All I'm saying is, it can take a while for people to change their thinking. There was a time, only about fifty years ago, when people didn't even think women should be allowed to vote. It took a lot of hard work for that to change."

"I know," said Julie with a sigh. She stared glumly at the floor. "I miss Ivy, though. It's not as fun without her."

"I bet she misses you, too," said Mom. "You're just going to have to give it a little time."

CHAPTER SIX

DUMPSTERS AND HOOPSTERS

Thursday morning, Julie woke up early with a tingling of excitement. She dressed and ate quickly. If she hurried, she could get the last three signatures on her way to school.

By the time Julie turned the corner at the bakery, she was almost running with eagerness to get to school—and Coach Manley. But she paused when she saw Hank drinking coffee through the bakery window. She walked over and pressed her clipboard up against the window. She held up one finger, then five fingers, then made a zero with her thumb and index finger. 1-5-0! Hank smiled a big grin and raised his coffee cup in a toast.

At school, Julie made a beeline for Coach

Manley's office. As she cut through the quiet gym, the smell of the polished wood and the squeak of her sneakers gave her goose bumps. She pictured herself faking left, driving toward the basket, and leaping in the air to make the perfect layup.

When Julie got to his office, Coach Manley was on the phone. She clutched the petition in her hands, waiting for the conversation to end. It was almost time for the bell to ring.

Standing in the doorway, Julie held the papers up, trying to get Coach Manley's attention. She shuffled her feet. She coughed. She was about to knock when Coach Manley motioned her in. Then he saw the papers in her hand.

"Whatever it is, Albright, just leave it," he told Julie, covering the receiver with one hand.

"But I . . . it's really—"

"I said leave it. Can't you see I'm busy right now? Stop back later."

Looking down at the rumpled, taped-together pages with curling edges full of smudged basket-balls, Julie thought of all she'd been through to get those hundred and fifty signatures. She wanted to explain the significance of all those names. But she had no choice. She set the papers down on Coach Manley's desk and rushed to her classroom as the bell rang.

✿

All day, Julie couldn't think of anything else. Finally, in the middle of social studies, she leaned over and whispered to T. J., "Do you think Coach Manley has read my petition?"

"Julie, T. J.?" said Ms. Hunter. "Is there something you'd like to share with the class about the Mississippi River?"

"Sorry, Ms. Hunter. I—I have a stomach-ache," said Julie, which wasn't exactly a lie. "May I please have a hall pass to go see the nurse?"

Julie started down the hall to the nurse's office, but she couldn't stop her feet from heading straight to the gym office. She knocked at the open door. "Excuse me, Coach Manley?"

"What is it, Albright? Shouldn't you be in class?" the coach barked.

"Did you get a chance to read my petition?" Julie asked, nervously twirling her mood ring. She was afraid to even look to see what color it was.

"I read it. Doesn't change a thing. Sports are for boys, not girls."

"But Coach, it's not just me anymore. A hundred fifty people agree that I have a right to play on the team."

"I don't care if you show me a hundred and fifty *thousand* names. They're all going in the same place." Right before her eyes, he balled up the petition and went for a basket … in the trash can.

Julie felt as if somebody had just punched her in the stomach.

"A piece of paper's never going to get you on this team," said the coach. "Now scram, before you get a demerit for being out of class."

As Julie headed back to her classroom, trembling with anger, a voice behind her boomed, "Young lady? Are you supposed to be in the halls right now?"

Julie stopped in her tracks. She turned and found herself looking right at Mr. Sanchez's pencil, which was pointing at *her* this time. His piercing eyes made her feel like a rabbit caught in an eagle's talons.

She held up her hall pass. "I'm on my way back to class," she squeaked.

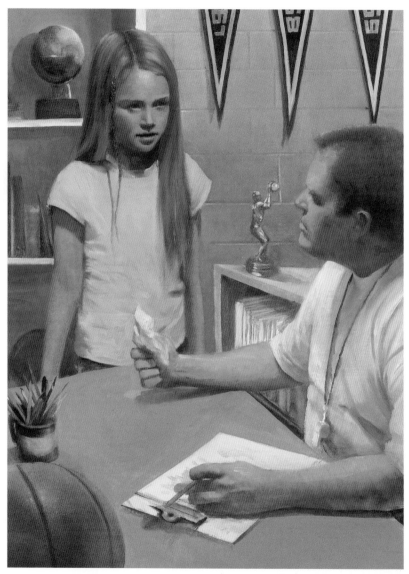

*"I don't care if you show me a hundred and fifty **thousand** names," said Coach Manley. "They're all going in the same place."*

"No wandering around now. Straight back to your lessons."

"Yes, Mr. Sanchez," Julie said, hurrying—but careful not to run—back to class.

❖

"I'm so mad, I could scream," Julie told T. J. as soon as the final bell rang. "All my hard work, and he just crunched up my petition like it was nothing but an old hamburger wrapper."

"What are you gonna do now?" asked T. J.

Julie paused. She'd been so certain her petition would work that she hadn't thought of a backup plan. There was only one thing she could think of to do. "Get my petition back."

"But how?"

"Come on. Let's go find Mr. Martin."

Mr. Martin, the janitor, was cleaning the cafeteria. He led them out the back door and gestured to seven giant bags of trash.

"They're ready for the Dumpster—but until then, they're all yours. Search away!" Mr. Martin said grandly, with a sweep of his arm.

Julie and T. J. dug right in.

For twenty minutes, they were up to their elbows in milk cartons, pencil shavings, Popsicle-stick projects, and old worksheets. When Julie looked up at T. J., his face was smudged with purple from all the ditto sheets. Ordinarily, Julie knew she would have laughed to see T. J. with a purple face, but right now she was too upset.

"I don't see it anywhere," said T. J. "And I better get to practice, or *I* won't be on the team either."

"Please, T. J. Only two more bags to go. Wait! What's this? Page two—this is it!" She held up the page in triumph. It was wrinkled and smeared with what looked like chocolate-milk drips, but Julie's heart leapt. It was like seeing an old friend.

They dug deeper into the bag. "Here's another page," said T. J.

"I found page one," said Julie. "We have them all. Even though they smell like sour milk. Thanks a million, T. J."

She knew what she had to do now. It would be harder than finding her petition in the trash, harder than facing Coach Manley, harder than collecting all the signatures. Ignoring her pounding heart, Julie made herself walk down the hall to the front office. But when she got there, she froze outside the forbidding door—the door that said Joseph Sanchez, Principal.

No turning back now, Julie told herself. The flutter inside her stomach was already whipping itself up into a tornado. She summoned all her courage and knocked on the door.

"Come in," a deep voice said.

Julie stepped into the principal's office, crossing the sea of gold carpet to stand in front of his desk, which was as shiny as a polished apple. Not even one paper clip was out of place. Julie stood flagpole-straight, clutching her petition. She felt her hands grow moist. *You haven't done anything wrong,* she reminded herself.

The principal looked up from his desk. "What can I do for you, young lady?" he asked.

Julie took a deep breath and began to talk. She told him about wanting to play basketball, and how there was only a boys' team and the coach said no girls. She told him how good she was at basketball, how her father always said she could dribble like a Harlem Globetrotter, but now that her parents were, well, divorced, she couldn't play very often with her dad anymore. Then, suddenly running out of words, she handed Mr. Sanchez the wrinkled petition.

The principal looked at the first page. Julie could hear the clock ticking as he read the long list of names. He turned to the next page, and the next. Finally, he peered over his reading glasses at Julie.

"So you're a hoopster. You know, I was a pretty good point guard myself, back in my high-school days. I used to dribble circles around some of the tallest guys on defense."

He wasn't angry with her! Julie felt herself breathe again.

"I can see this means a lot to you," Mr. Sanchez continued. "I can't make any promises, Julie. I'll have to talk this over with the school board. I'll get back to you next week."

❀

At home that evening, Julie gushed with news of her eventful day.

"I'm proud of you, honey," said Mom, putting her arm around Julie and squeezing her tight.

"Weren't you scared talking to the principal?"

asked Tracy.

"Yes," said Julie. "But he turned out to be nice. He used to play basketball, too."

Bling! The timer went off in the kitchen. Mom walked over to the oven and pulled out a steaming casserole.

"Anyone hungry?" Mom asked. "I made tuna noodle casserole. With potato chips on top, the way you girls like it."

"You made a real dinner?" Julie and Tracy asked at the same time, looking at each other in disbelief.

"Come on, it's not all that unusual, is it?"

"Mom, we've had takeout about a hundred times since we moved," said Tracy.

"Only a hundred?" asked Julie, and everybody laughed.

"Hey, Mom, don't forget. Tell her about the thing." Tracy nodded toward the table by the front door.

The *thing*? Nervously, Julie followed her sister's glance toward the front door, but she couldn't see anything unusual.

"Oops, I almost forgot in all the excitement," said Mom. "A package came for you today."

"For me?"

"Special delivery!" Mom winked at Tracy.

The small box was taped shut and rattled a little when Julie shook it. "It doesn't say who it's from," she said, puzzled.

"Just open it!" said Tracy.

Julie ripped open the box, only to find a paper-towel tube inside with the ends taped shut. She peeled the tape off one end and shook out a rolled-up sheet of paper that fell open like a scroll.

"What does it say, Jules?" asked Tracy.

"It's a petition," Julie said slowly. "Just like the one I made for basketball, with columns and numbers and everything."

At the top were big block letters. Julie read the words aloud: "Petition to Be Julie Albright's Best Friend. One–Ivy Ling. Two–Ivy Ling. Three–Ivy Ling. Four–Ivy Ling. Five–Ivy Ling . . ."

Julie unrolled the petition all the way to the floor. "She signed it one hundred and fifty times!"

"That's some friend you've got there," said Mom.

Monday went by without a word from
Mr. Sanchez. Then Tuesday. Every time Julie left
her classroom, she kept an eye peeled. This time,
instead of worrying that he'd point his accusing
pencil in her direction, she was actually hoping to
spot him, but Mr. Sanchez was nowhere to be seen.
On Wednesday, Julie offered to take the roll-call sheet
to the office for Ms. Hunter, just hoping that the
principal might come out from behind that closed
door. But he didn't.

Finally, on Thursday, shortly before the last bell
was about to ring, an announcement came over the
PA system. "Julie Albright, please report to the
principal's office. Julie Albright."

"What'd you do?" Angela asked.

"She's in trouble!" said Alison.

It was all Julie could do not to sprint down the
hall to the office. But at the same time, she could feel
a knot in the pit of her stomach, a small lump of
dread. What if the school board had turned her
down? What if the principal had talked to her dad?
What if the answer was *no?*

Mr. Sanchez was standing in the doorway to

his office. "Hello, Julie," he said, motioning for her to come in and sit down. He cleared his throat. "After careful consideration, I've determined that we're not in a position to start a girls' basketball team at this time." He paused. Julie's heart sank.

"However, I've also determined that to be in full compliance with Title Nine, our school must allow you to play on the boys' basketball team." He smiled. "So, that makes you the newest member of the Jack London Jaguars."

Julie jumped up out of her seat. She could hardly keep from throwing her arms around him. Wait till she told T. J.!

"Now, before you get too excited, I'm not finished yet. Let me stress that there may be some who will disagree with this decision, and I don't want any trouble, on or off the court. I've spoken with Coach Manley, and you will report directly to him if you have any problems."

Julie nodded. "Thank you, Principal Sanchez," she said politely. But in her mind, she was already dribbling down the hall, through the open doors of the gym, and out onto the court.

Walking home, Julie took a shortcut and realized for the first time that she knew the route by heart. She no longer had to concentrate on street names, landmarks, or left and right turns. Her feet practically bounced with the good news, past the purple iron gate, past the funny-face fire hydrant, past the giant peace-sign mural. She couldn't wait to tell Mom and Tracy, knowing how excited they'd be for her. Ivy, too.

Dad. Julie wondered what he would say. He hadn't liked the idea of her playing on a boys' team—but wasn't he the one who'd taught her how to shoot hoops in the first place? Surely he wouldn't really be unhappy.

Julie imagined bursting through the front door of their old house and announcing the good news to her whole family, all together, and then racing across the street to tell Ivy. Unfortunately, that's not the way it would be. She couldn't even call Dad tonight—nobody would answer the phone at his house, and she didn't even know where he was flying this week. She'd just have to wait and tell him on the weekend. That's how it was now. But she wasn't going to let it spoil her good mood.

As Julie turned the corner onto Redbud Street, she saw the welcoming lights beneath the front awning of Gladrags, glowing as if in celebration. Mom would be there, bracelets jangling as she arranged items on a shelf or waited on a customer. And Tracy would be home any minute, tossing her tennis racket on the kitchen table, kicking off her sneakers, fixing herself a snack. In the living room, the prism hanging in the front window would just be catching the last light of day, splashing rainbows everywhere, all around the room.

Julie broke into a run, heading home.

LOOKING BACK

AMERICA
IN THE
1970s

Katy Steding, above left, was the only girl on her youth league basketball team. She went on to play for one of the very first women's professional teams, the Portland Power. (That's Katy touching the ball, above right.)

When Julie was growing up, many people didn't think girls could do the same things boys did. They thought only boys should become doctors or lawyers or scientists or athletes. They thought sports, especially team sports like basketball, should be only for boys. Some schools didn't even have gym classes for girls.

But these views were beginning to change. Congresswoman Edith Green wanted to make sure that girls would have the same opportunities boys had at school. When Congress passed a law known as the Education Amendments of 1972, Edith Green included a section

Representative Edith Gree

forbidding *sex discrimination,* or unequal treatment of boys and girls, at schools that received money from the federal government—which included nearly every school in the country, from elementary to college. This section became known as Title Nine (often written Title IX).

At first, schools didn't realize how many changes Title Nine would require. They knew they were supposed to start paying female and male teachers equally and start admitting more female students into law, business, and medical schools. But two years passed before schools realized that the new law also meant they had to provide athletic teams for girls—or else let girls play on the boys' teams.

Jackie Adams, age 8, was one of the first girls to play with boys on a Little League baseball team.

One ten-year-old girl named Dot Richardson loved baseball but had no team to play on. So she helped her brother warm up for his Little League games by pitching balls to him. When the coach saw how well Dot pitched, he invited her to play. Since Little League didn't allow girls, he told her, "We're going to have to cut your hair short and give you a boy's name." But Dot didn't want to pretend she was a boy! After

Dot Richardson, shown here in 1972, grew up to become a surgeon.

Title Nine, she joined a girls' fast-pitch softball team and became one of the best players in the country.

In Julie's day, tennis was one of the few sports with professional women players, but compared with the male players they received little pay or respect. Tennis pro Bobby Riggs

Dot Richardson won a gold medal in softball at the 1996 Olympics.

claimed that a man could beat any woman on the court. In 1973, he challenged tennis pro Billie Jean King to a well-publicized match known as the "Battle of the Sexes." Because Bobby Riggs had proudly called himself a "male

Billie Jean King

chauvinist pig," Billie Jean King gave him a baby pig as a gift before the game started!

Despite the lighthearted atmosphere, Billie Jean had prepared hard for the match. She knew that if she lost, it would confirm what a lot of people thought: that females shouldn't be taken seriously as athletes. Billie Jean King creamed Bobby Riggs in three straight sets, sending a powerful message that female athletes could play just as well as men.

Sports wasn't the only arena in which attitudes about

In the 1960s, newspapers advertised jobs for women separately from the regular job openings, which were expected to be filled by men. The women's jobs did not pay as well.

women were changing. By the 1970s, girls were going on to college and graduate school in record numbers. As Title Nine opened more colleges and professional schools to females, more and more women became lawyers, doctors, business-women, and scientists—jobs that traditionally had been occupied by men. Many women simply wanted the satisfaction of doing respected, well-paid work. Others worked because they had to. In many families like Julie's, where the parents had divorced, women had to go out and earn an income, often for the first time.

Before the 1970s, divorce was quite rare. Since women had limited opportunities for work outside the home, leaving a marriage often meant great financial hardship. Besides, as Julie knew, getting divorced carried *stigma*, or a strong sense of public shame. Parents usually felt it was best for their children if they stayed together, even when their marriage wasn't happy.

Sally Ride studied physics in graduate school. In 1978, she joined NASA. She became America's first female astronaut.

But by the mid-1970s, women had more options. Many went back to school and got a degree or started a business, so they were no longer dependent on their husbands for income. When a couple found they had different ideas about how to live their lives, they sometimes chose to get divorced.

More and more women—including those who stayed happily married—started seeing

themselves as independent people with ideas and skills of their own. To make this point, some women stopped identifying themselves in the traditional way by their husband's name, such as "Mrs. John Smith." Instead, they adopted the title Ms., followed by their own name, "Ms. Susan Smith," whether they were married or single, just as Julie's teacher did.

*Gloria Steinem co-founded **Ms.** magazine, which focused on women's new roles and options.*

These social changes weren't easy. In the mid-1970s, when Julie's story begins, Americans were reeling from other major changes. They recently had watched President Richard Nixon resign over the scandal known as *Watergate*. The idea that their president had tried to cover up the burglary of files from his political opponents and then had lied to the public about it was shocking. The public was also deeply divided over their country's role in the Vietnam War. By the early '70s, a majority of people disapproved of America's involvement in Vietnam. Many Americans

People standing outside the gates of the White House, reading the news of President Nixon's resignation

lost trust and confidence in their government. It sometimes seemed as if all the time-honored American ideals were being turned upside down.

In the late 1960s and early 1970s, millions of people protested America's presence in Vietnam. It was the first time so many Americans had publicly opposed their government.

For Americans who wanted their world to stay the same as it had been, such profound changes—in their government, their jobs, their marriages, and even their sports—were upsetting. But other Americans, especially young people, welcomed the changes. They believed that creating a fairer society, where girls and women had the same opportunities as boys and men, would improve life for all Americans.

Title Nine created opportunities for talented players like soccer star Mia Hamm, whose team won the Women's World Cup in 1999.

A SNEAK PEEK AT

Julie
TELLS HER STORY

*Julie doesn't want to think about her school project.
It's a lot more fun helping Tracy with hers—until one
little mistake leads to disaster.*

By the way," Tracy said, absentmindedly curling a strand of hair around her finger. "You know how you've been dying to babysit?"

"Yeah, but Mom says I'm still too young," Julie replied. "Why? You know somebody who needs a babysitter?"

"Umm—sort of."

"Who?" Julie bolted upright, excited by the possibility of her first job. "When can I start? Do you think Mom'll let me? How much do they pay?"

"Well, since it's your first time, it would have to be for free. You know, to get experience. Then you work up to the big bucks."

"I don't know," said Julie, leaning back on her elbows. "On *The Brady Bunch*, Marcia and Greg get their parents to pay them just to babysit their own brothers and sisters."

"Well, this isn't *The Brady Bunch*," said Tracy. "Could you start later today?"

"You mean it? For real? How old is the kid? What's the kid's name?"

Tracy hesitated. She glanced sideways at Julie. "Charlotte?" she said, making it sound like a question.

"It's your spider plant!" Julie said in disbelief.
"You want me to babysit a dumb old plant?"

"C'mon, Jules, you'd really be helping me
out. Just go in my room and check on it a couple
times while I'm gone. If the soil feels dry, give it a
little water. And if you notice anything unusual, just
write it down, so I can record it in my science journal."

"I never heard of such a dopey idea—babysitting
a plant."

"Sure, it's called plant-sitting. You can make a lot
of money taking care of people's houseplants when
they go away."

"Plant-sitting, huh? Okay, I'll do it. But it'll cost
you. Two dollars."

"Two dollars! Are you nuts? For maybe watering
it once, and making sure it doesn't croak?"

"Take it or leave it," said Julie, crossing her arms
to show that her mind was made up.

"One dollar," said Tracy.

"Deal," said Julie.

❁

"The eensy, weensy spider went up the water spout,"
Julie sang to the plant on her bedroom windowsill.

91

Ivy joined in, adding all the hand motions that went with the song.

"Tell me again why we're singing to a plant?" Ivy asked.

"It's for Tracy's science project. She asked me to watch her plant this weekend, but I was afraid I'd forget, so I just brought it in here. There's more sunlight in my room, anyway," said Julie. "And I read in a magazine that if you sing to plants, or play music around them, they grow faster."

"Really? That sounds wacky," said Ivy.

"I know," Julie admitted. "But wouldn't it be great if Tracy came back and her plant had grown a whole inch? She'd get extra credit for sure. Let's sing it again!"

"Okay, one last time," Ivy agreed. "Then let's go do something outside."

"I know—this time I'll tape us singing!" said Julie. "Then I can just play the tape for Charlotte."

When the girls were finished singing, Julie pressed the play button and then picked up her basketball. "Want to go shoot some hoops?"

"Sure!" said Ivy. "Let me get my shoes on."

"Think fast!" Julie said, tossing a pass at Ivy. But

Ivy had bent down to tie her shoes. The ball bounced off the dresser, rattling Julie's gumball machine, then zinged off the floor, heading right for the open window.

"Noooooo!" Julie dove across the bed, lunging to save the ball from going out the window. The basket-ball thumped against the windowsill, then bounced into Julie's hands. "Whew—got it!"

Ivy stared at her in horror.

Crash.

"What was that?" Julie followed Ivy's gaze to the open window—and empty windowsill.

For a split second, Julie's mouth gaped open in shock. Then Julie and Ivy rushed over to the window and peered down at the sidewalk below. Charlotte lay in a jumbled heap on the ground. Dirt was scattered all over the sidewalk. The clay hippo was smashed to pieces.

In a blur, Julie and Ivy raced down the back steps and out onto the sidewalk.

"Oh, no!" said Julie, covering her face in disbelief. "What are we going to do?"